For my own chicks, Kate and Anna. Love always – E. B.

For Lucie, thanks for all your support. Don't get pooped on! – M. C.

Copyright © 2012 by Good Books, Intercourse, PA 17534
International Standard Book Number: 978-1-56148-769-1
Library of Congress Catalog Card Number: 2012000187

Text copyright © Elizabeth Baguley 2012
Illustrations copyright © Mark Chambers 2012
Original edition published in English by Little Tiger Press,
London, England, 2012
LTP/1400/0396/0412 • Printed in China

Library of Congress Cataloging-in-Publication Data
Baguley, Elizabeth.
Pigeon poop / Elizabeth Baguley ; Mark Chambers.
p. cm.
Summary: A perfect town is plagued by Pidge's trail of poop until
a young girl finds a way for pigeons and people to peacefully co-exist.
ISBN 978-1-56148-769-1 (hardcover : alk. paper)
[1. Stories in rhyme. 2. Pigeons--Fiction. 3. Feces--Fiction.] I. Chambers, Mark, 1980- ill. II. Title.
PZ8.3.B143Pig 2012
[E]--dc23
2012000187

Pigeon PooP

Elizabeth Baguley

Mark Chambers

Good Books

Intercourse, PA 17534, 800/762-7171,
www.GoodBooks.com

In a perfect town with spotless streets,

And flawless lawns with shiny seats,

A pigeon swooped and looped the loop,

And left behind a trail of . . .

Umbrellas, shoes,
and smart new hats

Were spoiled by Pidge's
splots and **splats**.

A silky dog who'd been all black
Was left with **spots** across his back.

A garden gnome was out of luck,

Some champion sunflowers dripped with muck.

When Pidge flew by he'd always drop

A massive load of pigeon **plop.**

As Pidge high-dived with loops and twists
The townsfolk frowned and shook their fists.
They stamped and shouted, full of rage:
"THAT PIGEON SHOULD BE IN A CAGE!"

They set a trap
to catch the chick

But clever Pidge
was far too quick.

Dedicated to those
who fell in the Great
Custard Battle of 1836....

He shot off to a
dizzy height
And turned a statue
gloppy white.

The townsfolk gathered
chains and strings,

Cogs and sprockets,
stretchy things.

They made a **whopping,**
Super-duper,
Snapping, zapping...

Instructions

With sparks and pops,
the **HUGE** contraption
Catapulted into action.

Pidge dodged
and dived . . .

and ducked
and flapped,
But soon, poor Pidge
was firmly . . .

But one girl cried, **"HE SHOULD BE FREE!**

I'll save our town—leave this to me!"

And soon our Pidge was clean and tidy

In a poop-proof . . .